I0562993

The Rage of Ogun

Clint Hulsey

Alternative Book Press
2 Timber Lane
Suite 301
Marlboro, NJ 07746
www.alternativebookpress.com

This is a work of fiction. All characters appearing in
this work are fictitious. Any resemblance to real people,
living or dead or otherwise, or locales is purely coincidental.

2014 Paperback Edition
Copyright 2014 © Clint Hulsey
Cover Illustration by CL Smith
Book Design by Alternative Book Press
All rights reserved
Published in the United States of America by
Alternative Book Press

Originally published in electronic form in the United
States by Alternative Book Press.

Publication Data
Clint , Hulsey, [date]
The Rage of Ogun/ by Clint Hulsey.—1st ed.
p. cm.
1. General (Fiction). I Title.
PS1-3576.C55H857   2014
813'.6—dc23

ISBN 978-1-940122-14-4
Printed in the United States of America
10 9 8 7 6 5 4 3 2 1

Table of Contents:

"Their rage supplies them with weapons"
-Virgil, Aenied

Chapter 1

The Cop threw the box in the back of the car somewhat haphazardly. With no lid on the box, a box that was clearly just pulled out of storage somewhere, most of the contents, mainly valueless keepsakes and pictures that he kept on his desk, something that he used as rarely as possible, spilled onto the floorboard as the box bounced on the back seat, hitting the back of the front seat and landing sideways between the two seats. He walked to the other side of the car and opened up the driver side, got inside slowly, and slammed the door behind him.

The car was an ugly, brown thing with a small engine and a high pitch whine that shrieked like an annoying child when he started it. He was a rather large man, and didn't fit in the car properly. He needed a car, but on his salary, his old, now non-existent salary, he couldn't afford a better one, and clearly, using a police car or a city-owned car was no longer an option. He would always think of himself as a cop, as the Cop, but officially, as far as the City was concerned, he was no longer one. He was called into the office of the Police Chief earlier that day, as the Chief wanted to speak to the Cop personally in an attempt to seem more human. The Cop didn't have a lot of respect for the Chief, a rather portly man with a cartoonish, red mustache and a bald spot large enough that he made sure to never reveal it through always wearing hats. Telling him that he had lost his job didn't give the Cop anymore respect for the Chief either. All the Cop heard was the words "cuts," a word he heard several times. They had to happen. Nothing could be done. It wasn't his fault the Chief insisted, and the Cop couldn't help but notice that the latter absolving of blame was much more emphasized, the denying of it being the Chief's fault was much more fervent than the denying of the firing, or cuts, being the Cop's fault.

As a man with experience, a man with a higher-than-average pay, and close to retirement, the Cop was one of the first to go when the City announced that it had needed, their words not his, to make "cutbacks" to the police force. To be fair, the police force was one of the last parts to be "cut," as the more general parts of the City government had suffered cuts long ago. The money was all gone he was told. The government couldn't keep their obligations. There were deficits that had been to be taken care of, ones that were bigger than just the city government, something that went to the state governments and the national government as well. There had to be cuts made, and he was one of them. "Cuts" was a funny word to the Cop, like he was an unwanted part of a piece of paper, like the scraps that were cut around, and discarded. Everyone also had their pensions reduced in recent years, part of the first round of "cuts ." The government was broke . So now the Cop was broke.

As he drove down the street, heading towards the interstate so he could make the approximately thirty minute drive, depending on traffic of course, to his small house at the edge of the City, the Cop felt an alarming amount of bitterness. The idea that he had been targeted, sought out so he could be exploited. You wouldn't know it if you were in the car beside him, going forward for a few feet before stopping, repeating the mindless and frustrating action in an almost infinite manner, because the Cop isn't the kind of man who betrayed his emotions. If you saw him, you would see a large, stoic man spitting into a cup, repeating a rather old, and a rather disgusting tobacco habit. He didn't even have road rage, calmly stopping and letting the more aggressive cars get in front of him. The way he drove did not reflect how he was feeling.

The Cop had been betrayed by the people that he once trusted and protected. The car had started to sputter, so he pulled over to the side of the interstate and parked in the ditch. He killed the car, and got out. He didn't know what to do, and he didn't know how to fix a car, so he angrily kicked it. He kicked the door, he kicked the tires, he kicked the front, and he kicked the back knocking out his own taillight.

Chapter 2

The Detective walked briskly up the stairs. Standing at about 6 feet high, the Detective wasn't an imposing figure, but he wasn't small either. He could certainly defend himself, but he didn't carry a gun most of the time. He usually worked on the scene, but he didn't fight or arrest criminals. Instead, he tried to figure out why and how crimes were committed. He was well-educated, and he fancied himself as a guy who used brain instead of brawn. In many ways, he could be considered a nerd or a geek, but his size, and his decision to wear contacts instead of glasses hid this. He was physically fit, he had a standard haircut, he wore a suit and jacket, and he carried a small briefcase in hand.

The Detective made it up to the third floor of the apartment building and saw where the alleged murder had occurred, thanks to yellow and black police tape roping off the scene. He ducked under the tape, noticing that the door of the room wasn't intact. It wasn't that it had been kicked in, but instead, it looked like it had been blown up. Splinters and pieces of the door covered the floor, and even the doorknob was in two different places.

"Anyone know what happened to the door?" the Detective asked.

"We are more worried about the body," a woman police officer replied condescendingly. The Detective ignored her. He didn't like working with regular police officers in the City, thinking of them as somewhat ignorant Neanderthals that had become increasingly likely to shoot their guns and ask questions later. The Detective stopped to inspect the pieces of the door lying all over the hallway. Clearly it had not been kicked apart, and it was very doubtful that anyone could do this wielding an ax. It seems that the knob had been blown apart, judging from some of the pieces appearing to be burned, like someone had made a homemade bomb that was only strong enough to do some damage, to possibly blow up a door, but not strong enough to start a fire in the room.

"Have you talked to anyone else on the floor?" the Detective asked, not directed at any particular officer.

"We did our rounds, we talked to everyone on the floor that was here when it happened, no one saw anything."

"But did they hear anything?" he asked.

"I am not sure?" the woman cop answered back in what could only be described as a question

"And what about the lobby, did anyone see him come into the apartment, and then get on the elevator?"

"I don't know, detective, but it doesn't appear there was a gunshot in here, at least we don't see a bullet wound or a casing, so I don't see what anyone would hear."

The Detective shook his head in disgust as he finally got out of the crouch and started to walk in to the room. There were four traditionally uniformed police officers in the room, three men and the woman, mostly standing around, as they had already looked throughout the apartment, finding very little of note. On the bar table of the apartment laid a lifeless body. It didn't just lay there though. The person, a male with above average but not overpowering size, had been stapled to the table, stapled so well that the police weren't sure how they were going to get the body off the table without significantly damaging or contaminating the evidence.

The blood indicated that the staples had penetrated his clothes, which remained relatively intact all things considered, and had pierced through the man's skin, holding him to the table. It appeared that he was stapled while he was still alive, at least this is what the blood indicated. Large exterior staples held the person to the table, and also seems to have ended his life, as the killer put one through his throat as well.

The puzzle was how the man had been put onto the table, how he was forced to get into the position to be stapled. The victim was muscular, the tattoo on his right arm suggested that the victim was a gang member. It had to be a group of people that did this. it couldn't have been just one person. The motivation for killing the man wasn't too difficult to pinpoint. Men and women die from gang violence every day. The Detective was more concerned with figuring out what could have motivated this killer to murder the man like this. Why would a gang, or anyone else, staple a man to a table while he was still alive?

The first thing the Detective did was check the man's hands to see if there was any evidence or a struggle or a fight, or if there was anything to glean as far as physical evidence from the hands or fingernails. Strangely, the hands had not been stapled to the to the table itself, but instead stapled to each other and stapled to the stomach area. They were badly damaged, but it was going to be nearly impossible to gather anything from them.

"Ever seen anything like this?" one of the officers asked the Detective.

"No. This is unusual even for gang violence," he answered, slowly, not looking up from the body. The place had not been robbed, and nothing other than the door had been disturbed.

Chapter 3

The Cop finally walked into his dark and empty apartment hours after he had left his job for the final time.

"Have a good day?" a strange voice greeted him sarcastically from another room, probably the kitchen. The Cop couldn't see where the voice was coming from, but he reached for his pistol in his jacket pocket.

"Don't bother," the voice said as the Cop heard a loud tapping sound coming from the other room, the sound of something metal thumping on something wood.

"What do you want?" The Cop asked as he paused in the doorway, taking his hand off of his gun, leaving it in his holster.

"You can sit down," the strange voice whispered with a slightly dry chuckle, "It is your house." The voice was raspy and while it was deep and distinctive, the Cop had a problem telling whether or not the voice was of a man or a woman thanks to almost robotic nature in tone and diction. The Cop fearfully sat on his couch, staring at his wall and turned off television somewhat blankly.

"I saw you kick your car today. I saw what they did to you." There was a pause, with the Cop sweating in the heat of his own house, not answering. The air conditioner in his house did not always work properly, and since he was a big man, he kept several fans throughout the house, usually on throughout the day so he didn't have to turn them on and off when he arrived or left the house. However, they were all turned off, and the intruder had not bothered to turn the air conditioner on, either. He wiped his forehead, and started breathing heavily, both because of fear and the heat.

"I am as angry as you are," the voice spoke again. "There is just so much pain and suffering in the world isn't there? So much exploitation, the proverbial sticking it to the little guy. It isn't just far away either isn't it? It is here, in the City, where everyone wants to live. The land of opportunity right? I just wish I could change things, sometimes I feel helpless -- like even if I do something --- it is impossibly small and fruitless in the grand scheme of things, like I will never be able to fix the City by myself. It is like I am building a wall – a wall I can never build in my lifetime – and I build it -- knowing that as soon as I die, someone bigger than me will kick it down, nullifying my entire life's work in mere moments. I am a bug living in a human's world, constantly being smashed, with a lifespan that is only long enough to start something, but never to finish them, long enough to recognize futility, but not long enough to embrace meaning. Do you know what I mean?" the intruder spoke to the cop as if they were engaging in a normal conversation, but normal conversations usually do not require breaking into someone's house.

"No," the Cop said.

"You worked for three decades as a police officer, didn't you?" the intruder asked. "Three decades putting away men and woman for doing all sorts of misdeeds, in an effort to stop misdeeds. Are there less misdeeds now than there was when you started? Have things gotten better? If not, were you just really incompetent, unable to find the people who kept doing misdeeds? Were you unable to unlock the puzzle that caused them to do it in the first place? Did the world become a better place because you were a cop?"

The Cop became metaphorically hot as well thanks to the insult. The word "cop" bothered many police officers, but not him. It was the implication that everything he had done in his life so far , had been pointless. The real insult was not some word that the intruder called him, or the fact that he was an intruder in his house. The insult was that the intruder called the Cop's life meaningless. The Cop believed fervently, that even if the people around him were bad or not as good as he was, he was doing good. What he did was important. He saved lives, he brought people to justice, he took down bad guys.

The intruder, continued: "It would be nice to be able to do something, wouldn't it? Something real, something meaningful, something that changes the lives of not only yourself, but those around you as well. That is what I want to do, and what I have been trying to do. To live life with meaning is what everyone wants to do. Countless generations of kids who became lawyers and firefighters grew up to be disappointed. There are always more fires, more people to sue. Nothing fundamentally changes, just the bugs building the wall, not quite realizing how incredibly pointless it is. Don't you want to change it?"

"How?" the Cop responded with one word. His anger showed through his heavy breath.

"By removing those who have taken away our choices," the intruder responded. "The ones that decided your future for you. You can, you are a trained killer. They taught you how to hunt and to end people's lives. But..." The intruder paused as the sound of the tapping continued and appeared to get louder.

Before the Cop could ask "but what?" the intruder in the other room continued. "The beauty is, you don't have to." The intruder's speech went on: "You can do whatever you want. It is all about choice. You can choose to build the wall, or you can choose to live for purpose and end the cycle of meaningless. I don't care what people do. I do care when other people are held down and forced to build the wall. I care when other people have the choices of their life taken away from them. I care when people are, say, let go without cause and have their futures taken away from them."

The voice paused, making it unclear if he was trying to tell a joke that wasn't very funny or just being very overt. "I choose to not accept it. See, I am what happens when people aren't given the choice."

"Who are you?" The Cop asked

"I am someone who needs you," the intruder replied. "You know what is wrong, and I am here so you will help me. I was created by the same kind of people who did this to you. They ruined my life, just like they ruined yours."

"It doesn't sound like I have a choice," the Cop said in a manner that made it clear that he was puzzled by exactly what the voice wanted.

"That isn't my fault," the intruder answered. I am not the one who took everything away. If you feel that you don't have a choice, that you have to take action, it isn't because of me." The Cop wasn't exactly so sure, but there was a pause. The Cop couldn't think of a response.

The voice continued "I'm Ogun, and I am...," Ogun took a slight pause, "I don't like this City. Guys like you aren't in charge anymore. The power has gone to people, or things, that don't allow others to make their own choices. People have been limited to what they can do. Isn't it odd that you were never placed in charge? Your record is quite impressive, and yet, you didn't get the big promotions. They kept you down, they oppressed you, and when they didn't need you anymore, they got rid of you, tossing you aside like a dirty dishrag. They will do anything for power and money, they are vultures and hoarders, but you, you know this. I was created by their evil, I live and act because of their evil, and at the same time, I am not nearly as angry as you are."

"What do you propose I do?" the Cop responded, almost whimpering.

"When people feel they have been wronged, they sometimes act in ways that are beyond even my imagination," the intruder said. Not initially satisfied with the answer and clearly wearing with a confused look on his face, the Cop stood up, to see if the intruder would notice. The tapping, the background music of the entire meeting had stopped. He heard a creak, thanks to his old back door, so the Cop took a couple of quick steps to the kitchen, with his hand back on the pistol in his holster. He paused, and when he no longer heard the voice, he continued into the kitchen. There was no one there, and very little evidence that anyone had been in there. The Cop tried to run out the door, to see if he could catch a glimpse of the intruder leaving his back yard, but to no avail. The Cop quickly packed up his bags.

The strangest thing about the murder of the gang member in his own apartment to the Detective was that all of the deceased persons' belongings were still in his pockets. His keys, his phone and his wallet, which still had not only money in it, but his ID as well, were all still in his pants. With the ID, the Detective was easily able to identify the victim with a simple search, and the dead man had indeed been very busy in his lifetime. Busted on a number of drug and gun charges, it was amazing that the man wasn't in prison. The man probably would love to be in a prison cell right now. No fingerprints were left in the apartment, no notes, or any other kind of indicator, so there were no real leads on the case.

Obviously, the man had not died from a gun shot wound, and from evidence gathered in the sweep of the apartment, there was no evidence a gun had been fired at all, meaning that, considering the guns that the man did have in his apartment, the act was sudden, since he was never able to fire a shot. The door being smashed to pieces suggests that he wasn't snuck up on, so it must have been someone who moves fast.

With this in mind, the Detective conjectured that it was some kind of professional killing. The crime was something not done by a traditional gangster, whose crimes were usually done a little more messy, and usually with guns. It may have been a hit put on by gangsters, though they often liked to do the work themselves, and they would have just used guns. This killing was tribal in nature, where the killer deliberately wanted other people to see this man and see exactly how he was killed.

"What did you get yourself into?" the Detective whispered to the lifeless body while standing over it. Surveillance tape at the apartment was no help. The cameras that were set up showed no one, and for some reason, there was no camera in the elevator or on the staircase.

Chapter 4

The Cop saw the Politician get out of his car. The car not fit for the average Public Servant. The Cop could never have afforded that car. In fact, he wasn't sure he could have afforded the paint job. It wasn't just that the Politician had one nice car. No, what really angered the Cop is that the Politician had three cars. Three really expensive cars. And a big house. And a wife that was a decade younger than him. The Cop on the other hand, drove his lackluster car to his small, empty house. The Politician didn't have these things ten years ago. Not until he got into the "Business" and then politics. The Cop wasn't sure what the "business" was, but it was something he always had a watchful eye on when he was a police officer. The Cop never had this life, and that is what angered him, almost to the point of pure, and perhaps petty, jealousy.

The Politician was no better than him. In fact, the Cop was convinced that he was quite worse. Like the intruder said, he had taken away the Cop's ability to choose, so he was about to do something unfathomable. He was about to take away the Politician's ability to choose. The Cop gripped his rifle, laying on his stomach on top of a building. He had never done this before. He had shot a gun before. He had shot this rifle more times than he could count. He had even shot people before. He had, after all, been a police officer in the field for about three decades in a major city with a serious crime problem. He just hadn't done this before. He has never killed anyone that wasn't holding a gun as well. After fiddling with his scope for several minutes and checking the wind patterns, he finally was ready to do the deed.

He still believed fervently, even after he pulled the trigger, that he had still never killed anyone that didn't deserve to die. This was the Politician who introduced the cutbacks that lead to the Cop's early retirement. This was the man who voted to cut the

Cop's pension. This was the man who insisted that the pensions of public employees couldn't be funded like they had been promised and that they had paid into. In some sense, the Politician ruined the Cop's life, so the Cop ruined the Politician's life. By ending it, effective immediately.

Chapter 5

"No motive, no suspect" the Detective muttered, looking at the dead body of the Politician. The mortician dryly replied that the victim was a politician and that by definition it wasn't really a mystery why anyone would kill him. They just didn't have any evidence as to who it actually was. The Detective didn't have the same sense of humor and didn't even glance up at the mortician. The body laid in a drawer next to other drawers with other dead bodies in it.

The Detective was not cognizant of the fact that in those drawers were other people who had sons, daughters, spouses, parents, and loved ones. It wasn't that he didn't know, he was after all, in a morgue, it was that the words "he's a politician," with the obvious implication that he was some kind of scumbag, didn't really rattle in his mind. While the Politician was the most high profile body in the morgue, it was entirely possible that he was the least valuable, at least in moral fiber. The irony didn't quite strike the Detective, at least not in the obvious way it did the mortician. The autopsy had already been done, and really found no results other than the obvious, the Politician died, almost instantly, from a single gunshot wound from a distance from a bullet that came from a gun that wasn't exactly common, but wasn't exactly custom made or illegal either.

The Detective paused for a long time. The mortician had left, and there was an indescribable silence in the room, as if it was filled not just with dead people, but with nothing. No politician in the City had ever been murdered, especially not assassinated from a roof top like he was some kind of president or king. This was clearly the biggest case of the Detective's career, but he didn't think about this either, his mind was focused on one thing: figuring out who did this and then why.

Chapter 6

The Cop had never taken drugs before. Nor had he ever ridden in a roller coaster. But supposedly, this is what taking drugs felt like, or at least, this was the feeling that teenagers got from riding a roller coaster. The rush of adrenaline was unparalleled to anything he had ever felt before. He was not usually someone fancied himself as a deep thinker, but the time alone since the first shooting had given him some time to think. He believed that the intruder was right, that the difference was choice. He made his own choices. Choices about where he goes and what time he had to be there, choices about what he did, and perhaps most important, choices about who lived and died. He got to make the choice as to who was worthy, and who was not. Perhaps the killings were ironic considering that the intruder's main problem seemed to be that people were having choices made for them, and the Cop was making choices about when people's lives ended.

He didn't see the irony, at least not as a problem, and the intruder's message wasn't exactly a peace keeping mission to the politicians, gangsters, and dirty police officers. He was the authority, and he was a good authority, unlike those that he killed. They were authorities, but they clearly were authorities with bad intentions. Even with the good intentions, the Cop had become an addict, and it didn't seem like he could stop.

He went to the house of a known gangster, one that he had tangled with before, one that had fired a gun at him before, and gotten away with it. He broke a window, climbed in, and walked into the bedroom, putting the gangster's spare pillow over his face, and pulling the trigger before the gangster could move, make a noise, or even gasp for air. The Cop had a silencer on his pistol, and it was 3 AM. No one would hear, and no one would know for quite a while. He pulled the trigger two more times, then another, and then, another. The only reason the Cop quit firing the gun was because he had eventually shot all the rounds in the clip. He calmly walked out of the house, putting his black heavy duty gloves, along with his pistol, back into his coat pocket. He was his own dispenser of justice.

Chapter 7

"So it's gangs?"

"It appears so, two gang deaths in a week."

"Yeah, but what about the politician?"

"Separate incident?"

The other officer's belief that the deaths in their own homes was purely gang related and that the politicians death was something unrelated didn't sit right with the Detective. First of all, gangs got rid of bodies, or at least hid them. They usually didn't just go to someone's house, murder them, and then leave their bodies there. The gangs in the City had a knack for burning bodies, or hiding them in dumpsters. Also, the gangs were pretty apolitical. They didn't influence politicians, much less murder them. As far as he knew, they didn't even try to bribe the police. For them to suddenly kill one of the most influential politicians in the city didn't make a lot of sense.

The Politician had not even been a big opponent of gang violence, fitting on the more libertine side, not wanting to increase police influence. If anything, it was the police that hated the Politician, not the gangsters. The Police Chief, not agreeing with the Detective's pleas to reconsider, sent the SWAT teams into a neighborhood that was known for breeding gang violence. It was a typically poor neighborhood, just outside the neighborhood where the gangster had been stapled to a table, and one that was accustomed to the background noise of misdeeds, drug deals, and gunfire.

The Chief believed that if he attacked the gangs, going after the leaders of the gang, he could not only find out the cause of the new rash of murders, but he could take the teeth out of the gangs in the City as well. He wanted to take down the gangs once in for all, or at least weaken them as much as he could.

The Police Chief wanted a fight, and that is what he got. The police and SWAT teams targeted 5 houses with known gangsters living inside. Two of the houses, with just a couple of people in them each, went down easily, with the men surrendering rather quickly. However, the other houses proved to be problematic, and realized the worst fears of the police officers on the mission. The people inside the houses decided to fight back. There was a reason they weren't already in prison, despite breaking the law quite regularly. They weren't going to go out without a bang. The police had escalated, so the gangsters did as well.

Even by the neighborhood's standards, the street had turned to violence and chaos. When the police tried to get an answer at the door at the front of one of the targeted houses, they got no answer. They continued to beat on the door, as a few of them ran to the back to surround the house and make sure none of them escaped. The authorities eventually knocked down the door, separating the hinges from the door frame by using a battering ram. If that was out of a tale from Ancient Greece, the next moment was out of the Wild West, as half a dozen gangsters squatting behind now overturned furniture fired wildly at the place where the door used to be.

The first SWAT member through the door was shot by at least a dozen bullets, with the vest stopping many of the bullets. However, it didn't stop one, which came straight to his heart. His body fell and stopped, blocking the doorway, and causing the second SWAT team member to trip and fall into the room, where he was quickly lit up with bullets. The two SWAT members behind the first two, stuck their rifles through the door, leaving their bodies pinned up to the left and the right of the door, up against the wall. They unleashed sprays of bullets that tore apart the furniture the gangsters were hiding behind, and would soon tear apart the men themselves.

The two officers coming from the back door finally opened it, only to find a gang member with a shotgun hiding to the left of the door with a shotgun. The man fired the shotgun as quickly as he could, knocking both SWAT members off their feet. However, moving to the front of the door exposed him through the hallway, and a stray bullet from the SWAT members from behind hit him right in the back, knocking him forward and causing him to crumple to the ground in agonizing pain, evidenced by his cries and moans. Now, most of the men inside the house were hit, with at least two of them being dead. It appeared that the SWAT teams were overpowering the gang members and would secure the house, until something else happened.

There really wasn't a rival gang in the neighborhood, it was basically one large gang, with a lot of sympathizers. The average person in the general area was scared of the gang, as they often terrorized the neighborhood, and predictably pressured poor people, especially kids and young adults to do favors for them, usually highly illegal favors, in exchange for money. Because of this, the police really had no idea who was not in the gang and who was. However, by attacking them, they were about to find out. There were four SWAT team members left outside the house that was now ravaged with bullets. Two of them had their backs turned, looking at the door, making sure that no one came out, if the two officers still at the door weren't enough, with the other two watching their backs, to make sure they weren't attacked from behind. It was pretty evident that the four weren't enough.

A man walked down the right side of the street, the opposite side of the street the SWAT teams were located. One of the SWAT members saw the man walking down the street, a somewhat skinny and tall man, walking with a clear limp.

"Freeze," was what the man heard, "shoot" is what the man did, pulling out a large machine gun and firing wildly towards the house. The SWAT members ducked behind their large vehicle and started firing back at him. Not worried about taking cover, the man was shot pretty quickly and taken down, firing his weapon into the air as he fell.

"Cover me," one of the two SWAT members behind the car yelled at the other. He walked briskly, with gun pointed at the body now at the ground while he walked towards him, while the other SWAT member, almost panicking, looking around for anyone else. Moving his gun around to his left and right, he had to make sure no one else was coming, that is, that the machine gunman was working alone. He wasn't, and the man's heart sank as the SWAT member getting to the body suddenly jumped at the same time as the sound of a gunshot rang throughout the street. The SWAT member then saw him, rather her, a heavily tattooed woman holding a pistol, firing uncontrollably. With a controlled burst by the officer behind the car, the woman was dropped. He knew that the man he was supposed to cover was shot at least twice, and he made his way towards him, crouching, walking as fast as he could without running, and looking every which way.

More shots rang out, and he ducked for cover, laying on the ground. The rest of the SWAT members that had surrounded the house but were still standing, ran towards the wounded SWAT member and the one laying on the ground. Using a series of hand motions, they split up and started to head towards houses, looking for the latest shooter. Getting close to the houses proved to a bad idea, as windows proved to be a good place for shooters to hold their guns out and shoot at the officers from close range. The situation had gotten out of control, even according to the most pessimistic projection for what was going to happen that day. They had in some sense unleashed a monster, trying to take down a whole gang at once.

The streets had closed down, not that anyone would want to drive in them anyway. Several of the surrounding blocks were roped off by police and many of the surrounding houses had been evacuated, at least the ones that would evacuate willingly. The middle of the street where the gunfire had started had become a disaster area, with bodies, both lifeless and wounded, strewn across the street like some child had thrown its toys about and then colored parts of the road with red crayon.

Three more police cars arrived at the scene, with more en route, driving on the parts of the street they could. Since the street was still somewhat of a battlefield, the authorities didn't want to send ambulances in, so the newest officers were, while equipped with rifles that they could use if necessary, mainly on a rescue mission for the wounded. They were looking for police officers that were wounded, trying to get them out of the area, and to the ambulances that were near.

One of the officers in the car saw someone moving near the curb ahead and instructed her partner to slow down. With his rifle firmly in her hands, he stepped out of the squad car when it stopped, pointing his rifle forward, looking both to his left and his right as the sound of gunfire further in front of him rang through her ears. She remembered, for a split second, the time at a gun range where people were all firing their weapons and she took off her ear muffs. This is the only sound that reminded her of what was going on around her, a deafening roar, except this time, there wasn't just the smell of powder and hot metal. This time, there was the sound of death, the sound of people crying out, the sudden end to at least a couple dozen lives, some of them just innocent bystanders.

She walked up to a police officer that was laying on the ground, but clearly moving, writhing and moaning in pain. The uniform showed that he had been shot at least a few times, and the blood and pain showed that at least a couple of the bullets had gone through the vest and gotten him. She desperately looked for the actual wounds, tearing apart his uniform. The man was babbling incoherently and wasn't a lot of help and finding the trouble spots. She eventually found them, one in the chest area, one in the stomach, and another possible one in the side. The officer was losing a lot of blood, so she desperately tried to use the ripped up uniform to press down and stop the bleeding. Unfortunately, she had lost total awareness of her surroundings, zoning in on saving the man's life.

"Watch out!" her partner screamed, with his head hanging out of the squad car window. This was the last thing she heard, as a spray of bullets hit her in the face. Her partner had been unable to pull the trigger on his pistol pointing out the side of the car, before she was shot by a gang member with a machine gun. The partner spotted the killer and fired the entire clip of his pistol, hitting the man several times and causing him to hit the ground as well.

With his partner presumed dead, he grabbed his rifle from the seat and found himself running from the squad car recklessly, pointing his rifle everywhere, desperately looking for something to shoot. He saw movement in windows, so he shot the windows. When something moved down the street, he shot that too, not caring about the affiliation, whether neutral, antagonistic, or even friendly, of the other side of his gun fire.

A classic car, with unnaturally large tires, illegally dark tinted windows, and an expensive paint job suddenly drove on to the scene, coming from behind a house directly in front of him. The car drove past the police officer before he could even pull the trigger, but he did see both sides of the car crack their windows, and hang guns outside of the window and fire at the two other police cars that had arrived at the scene just minutes before. This caused one of the squad cars, presumably because the driver had been shot, to swerve dramatically, and slam into the curb hard. No one was in the other police car, as they had already gotten out to help the wounded and get in more strategic fighting positions.

The officer fired his rifle rapidly at the car that was quickly driving away from him. The car then stopped, and the officer knew he had just 4 bullets left in his rifle. He fired one while it was stopped. The car then made it clear that it was planning on turning around and temporarily parked horizontally, so the person in the passenger seat of the car could fire its machine gun at the police officer. It was as if the only people in the universe was whoever was in the car and the police officer, an unattractive, somewhat rugged man who normally had an attitude that was much more appealing than his physical appearance. Today however, the ugliness came out in the form of a high powered rifle. The officer fired another shot. Two shots left. The machine gun kept firing at the officer, but none of the rounds were very close, as the gangster didn't use controlled bursts and was too far away in range for the gun to be accurate, especially considering how the gun was being held. The officer took a deep breath, and looked into the sights of his rifle. Aiming at the now reloading man with the machine gun in the car ahead, the officer pulled the trigger. One shot left and there was no longer a living and breathing man in the passenger seat. The car then backed up, with a real lack of caution, backing up over a curb, and turned around, driving directly at the officer. The driver, with one hand on the wheel, tried to fire his gun out the window at the officer, but the bullets were coming nowhere close to him, as if the driver forgot that he was holding a machine, not a magical spell that would land directly without any effort. Again, the officer readied his gun, aimed carefully, and prepared to pull the trigger.

Time was running out, he had to pull the trigger soon, as the car was about to run him directly over at a fatal speed. The hum of the engine getting louder as the car picked up speed didn't distract him, neither did anything else that had happened over the past half hour since he arrived. He pulled the trigger. No bullets left. The gun was empty, and now worthless against the oncoming car with the determined driver. It was over.

The bullet had hit the driver directly in the chest, causing him to involuntarily react and turn the wheel sharply. The car veered off from the direct path towards the officer that it had been on, and instead, jumped a curb to the right, and spun out in someone's yard. A young man, sensing that the commotion was getting too close to the house that he lived in, which was just a house down from the yard the car had wrecked itself into, opened his front door and ran the opposite direction, going from hiding to just trying to get out of the neighborhood.

The officer saw the young man, clearly unarmed, and ran him he down. He was in good shape, he made sure he worked out frequently, while the young man was a sixteen year old who liked to play video games and hadn't run in quite some time. The officer started beating him, with the butt of his gun as hard as he could right in the face, as the young man screamed for help, bloodcurdling screams that were heard by no one.

The young man had at least gotten to the middle of the street, finding himself tripping over a couple of bodies that had been slain in the shootings. One of the wounded neighborhood residents tried to grab onto the officer's pants, as much as a plea for help as to cause harm. The officer withdrew the pistol from his left holster, the pistol he had not fired yet, with his right hand and swung his arm to put the pistol up to his head and pulled the trigger, ending his life immediately. The woman came from her house to stop the police officer from beating the man, or in reality, the kid. The mother came to intervene between her sixteen year old son, that she didn't want to leave the house in the first place, and the police officer that was savagely beating him. The kid knew nothing, about anything really, much less anything about the recent attacks and murders. He wasn't even really part of the gang. He had nothing to do with the death of the partner of the officers death, nothing to do with the stapled man on the table, nothing to do with the death of the Politician, or the death of the SWAT team members who arrived in the neighborhood first and were a part of the beginning of the shootout. The kid had nothing to do with anything, but that didn't matter to the officer. The police officers took in the bloody kid, but he would die the next day.

The shooting of the gangsters was one thing, the war declared on them by the Police Chief would have angered the gang as a whole and caused a larger push back, but the killing of the kid caused them to become more violent against authorities than they ever had before, making the shootout look tame by comparison in terms of vengeance. The gang believed in their code, and believed that the kid was one of their own. While not usually the embodiment of moral fiber, the gang decided that they were going to take up the cause of the kid, fighting back against the police who killed him in the first place.

This meant war. The next police officer that set foot on the street was shot, and so was the next one. And like that, it became a war. The military was quickly brought in to combat the gangs. Not tanks or Marines, but National Guard members with machine guns. They quickly squashed what appeared to be the gang rebellion, by rounding up the gang members after a small skirmish showed that the gangs were over matched.

Chapter 8

The Cop's next target was nearly a walking cliché, but at the same time, a lot of what was wrong with the City. The Cop's target was a police officer, a high ranking one, but one that was taking money to allow illegal guns come into the city. He was cunning, though sometimes controlling and reckless. He had made sure on numerous occasions that the Cop wasn't able to do his job, especially when it came to finding, arresting, and provide evidence against some of the most prominent gang members, especially when it came to gun violence.

This time, the targeted police officer was meeting with a couple of gang members by the largest storage bin facility in the City, presumably taking money, straight out of a crime novel that the Cop would never read. The Cop was perched up on top of an old two story building, a vantage point that gave him a good look at the three people by the storage buildings from a northeast angle. The wind was blowing rather significantly, so he knew that it wouldn't be a very easy shot. Luckily, he could fire this rifle very quickly, and he had a large magazine that allowed him to use a large amount of rounds without reloading.

If he had to, he would use them all to remove the three men below from the earth. He pulled the trigger once, twice, three times, four times, again and again, until not only all three bodies were on the ground, but until they quit moving. He then calmly packed up his gun, first taking off the muzzle, and putting it into a hard cased bag, followed by the butt of the gun, until he had put all of the gun in the bag. He was in no hurry, no one could hear the shot, and he didn't see how anyone would have seen him get on the roof in the first place. He was also laying down on the roof, with a cover over him, and there were no tall buildings on the block.

This time, he felt, nothing. Instead of the rush he felt in previous killings, and the adrenaline he felt when he was with the police force, he felt something he couldn't describe. He was convinced, that he felt nothing, that at some point, he had lost the ability to feel. That the anger, followed by his actions, his killings of those that he had felt deserved it, had made him numb in some way. He didn't feel for his victims. He remembered that when he was working for the police, that they had a word for people like this, criminals that did extremely horrifying things and didn't seem to show any remorse. The Cop who had a friend that called those kind of people psychopaths.

Chapter 9

The CIA, brought in because of the nature of the assassinations, thought the gangs knew something. If they weren't behind the killings, and gangs usually were not behind the killings of politicians, then they knew who was behind the killings. This suspicion became a little more warranted after the arrests the CIA reasoned after remaining gang members seemed to come into some new weaponry.

"So you are telling me you know nothing? You don't know why the gangs were prepared for the raid, you don't know why the Politician was killed, and you don't know who did it?" screamed the CIA agent. One of the other agents put a small, thin cloth over the accused gang member, while another member poured water out of a jug onto his face, causing the African American man to choke and gag. "Do you still know nothing?" the agent standing a few feet from the dangled legs of the gang member sneered. The gang member started blurting out a mixture of obscenities and nonsense, looking for the magic word to stop what was going on.

"He isn't talking," one of the CIA agents said dryly to the other, stating the obvious. There was an a pause as the leading CIA agent stewed in his own anger. "Stop it. I hope like you prison, and the needle" he said to the gang member who was gasping for air.

Police responded to a burglary call in the neighborhood, cases which tended to be fruitless, because if the people inside had called, and unless there were gunshots, the call usually wasn't a neighbor, the robbers were already gone. Since robbers usually wear some kind of mask, especially ski masks, it was nearly impossible to get an identity on them, even assuming someone witnessed the robbery inside the house. Large men with broad shoulders usually wasn't good enough of a description to narrow down any list of suspects. Not to mention that many times, even if the robbers weren't masked, the descriptions given by people, especially scared victims, usually weren't very helpful. The only reason that the police would really respond to robberies in the City would be, to put it frankly, make the victims feel better that something was being done, and to make sure no one was injured. The squad car's seats were filled by two officers, long time partners, both of them males in their late 40s. They drove down the street, a street that was still torn apart by the warfare from the past couple of weeks, planning on meeting with two squads that had been on permanent duty on the nearby streets since the battles. However, they were not able to contact either of the other squads on their scanner.

The police officer in the passenger seat, convinced the equipment wasn't working, angrily banged the handle into the dash three times.

"Whoa," the driver yelled, appalled at the sudden outburst of anger from his partner, giving the other one a puzzled look, taking his eyes off the road.

When both of the police officers looked forward again, they saw smoke billowing into the sky. The house was still another block away, so their view was obstructed from seeing the house, but the smoke was clearly coming from that direction. The police officer in the passenger seat grabbed the now broken handle of the scanner and tried to speak into it, trying to relay that there was a fire in the area, giving the address.

The police officer got an answer, which only worried him further, as the police car, now with lights and sirens on, quickly turned the corner and pulled up to the house that was reportedly robbed, and was now engulfed in flames. If the scanner was working, even with his admittedly counterproductive smashing of the device, and he could reach others, then something was wrong with the officers that were actually in the area that he couldn't reach. Ever the optimist, he reasoned that maybe something was just wrong with their scanners, but he was frankly lying to himself. Both squad's scanners would have to be broken, something that simple odds wouldn't support, and the other squads were not at the scene of the fire, which if they were in the area, is where they would almost certainly be.

As the driver of the patrol car quickly parked, running up the curb slightly two houses down and across the street, to not get in the way of firefighters when they did arrive, the police officer in the passenger's seat sat in in both a shock and a daze.

The driving officer was already out of the car, hand on his holster where his pistol rested, jogging in the direction of the fire. The other side of the scanner acted somewhat shocked at the report of the fire and clearly acted as if the reporting by the two officers was the first they had heard about it. The officer, still in the passenger seat, looking up from the window at the small two story house burning muttered, with no one listening, "no one is coming out of that alive."

As he finally started to open the door and get out of the car, with his partner staring back at him bemused, wondering what was taking him so long, the police officer noted that there was something odd about this situation. In fires such as this, the police's job was to contain, mainly, make sure that there was space for the firefighters to do their work. The problem was, there were no onlookers. The police officer didn't have a ton of experiences with fires, but he knew that the general rule would be, just like with a nasty car crash in the middle of a town, there would be plenty of interested onlookers. No one was outside, save for one kid, probably no more than eight years old, on a bicycle, several houses down. The officer finally got out of the car and started walking briskly towards the child, not running towards him to make sure the kid wouldn't be scared.

"Where is everyone?" demanded the officer to the kid, who despite the officer's best intentions, looked very scared. "I am not supposed to talk to you," screamed the kid, trying to ride his bike away. Eventually he fell over, and got up, just running away, leaving the bike behind.

The officers, wondering where the rest of the neighborhood was, split up. One officer went to the house to the right of the fire to make sure the family in that house had evacuated as the fire seemed to be spreading to the other houses. The other officer moved to the house on the left, somewhat paranoid and shaking while holding a hand on his pistol. The flames from the other house nearly burned his face as he knocked on the door, causing his eyes to water. He patted down his hair to make sure none of the fire was in his hair. He was balding, and his hair looked pretty mediocre, but he certainly didn't want it on fire. No one came to the door, even when he knocked three times, but it was unlocked, so he opened it.

The police officer walked through the door, with his gun drawn. He saw someone above, someone on the stairway, appearing to be holding some kind of hose, not the end of it, but like he was holding it for someone else. The grizzled police officer, with much more hair on his face than any man should have, pointed his gun at the person above and demanded that they put their hands in the air. He then heard a noise, coming from his left, and he quickly turned around, only to feel a searing pain throughout his midsection, and then his face. It was like he had been stung by a bee, only much worse. He should have felt more pain, but his body hadn't quite caught up to what was happening, it had fallen into almost instant shock as the nails pierced his body, and as he fell, a fall from which he would never get up, a distraught woman looked over him, holding a nail gun with the safety removed.

Chapter 10

The Cop's hiding spot had been found out, but not because of anything the CIA had done, something that the Cop was also not aware of. He intentionally had not been back to his apartment since the meeting with Ogun. He didn't know it, but no one else had been either. No one suspected him, and honestly, most had already forgotten about him. When his hiding spot had been found out, it wasn't known by police who he was, the police just thought that they had caught the one who had been terrorizing the City.

The Cop was found out thanks to an anonymous tip in the Hotel room. A concerned, if not a little nosy, visitor two rooms away had noticed his strange luggage, and some of the strange sounds coming from his room. He then heard a particular noise, while out in the hallway in the afternoon. The visitor nearly called the lobby for the Hotel manager to report the noise but decided against it. He went back to his room, with the bottle of soda out of the vending machine and turned on his TV. He didn't get to go to the City very often, and while he was mostly there on business, he was not very busy, with only the occasional meeting during the week he was there. Instead of going and visiting around the City, he was lazy and just wanted to watch TV.

When he flipped on the TV, the news was on. He wasn't the kind of guy who watched the news, but it was a breaking report about someone being murdered almost directly under the hotel, in the street. The woman reporter, speaking a little quickly, having some problems simultaneously gathering all the data necessary to give a report and continue to speak in complete coherent sentences with the pressure of live television combined with the pressure of getting possibly a career story right, or at the very least, not getting it embarrassingly wrong. Perhaps one could say that the thought that someone had just died, that their life had ended and that they had family and importance to at least someone, was eerily far away for the woman.

Perhaps the thought that a sniper, the word she used, was probably in a building nearby, was also strangely not on her mind. It must have been the adrenaline coursing through her body, or the focus of doing a job well, or maybe even sheer bewilderment. Death, both the fear of, or the lamenting of a life ended, even if she didn't know him, was not on her mind. The visitor in the hotel room had none of this on his mind. The president, instead of the young blond woman on television, could have been delivering the report and the visitor's reaction would have been the same. The report could have been in Spanish, and as long as the visitor understood the words "sniper" and "death," he would have done the same thing. Before he was even conscience of it, the visitor had picked up the hotel phone beside the bed and dialed the numbers 9-1-1.

The Cop quickly knew that he had been found out. It was stupid to take the shot from his hotel room. He heard bustling in the hallway. He knew they were evacuating the people on the floor, he heard the hushed voices, the stampeding, and the running. He then heard the knock on his doorway.

He sat at the end of his bed, that was fully made and tucked in, not moving. The rifle was still in the window, and a machine gun laid in his lap.

The knocking grew harder and louder, impossible to ignore, like someone playing the drums, or the loud tapping noise that he once heard in his house the last time he was there, the sound of metal on wood that the intruder made. There were clearly two men, and one of them shouted something, directed at the Cop, but he wasn't paying enough attention to hear what they said. The television was off and his room itself was quiet. He sat in silence. He knew he had to do something. The question was what. He could easily take the two security guards, if not physically, with ammunition.

They weren't the problem. The problem is that more police officers would come. He couldn't fight an onslaught of infinite police officers like they were zombies mindlessly coming after him. This wasn't a video game, not that the Cop had ever played one. He needed to gain leverage somehow. He had been on the others side of hostage situations. Situations where he had felt powerless. He remembered one such situation somewhat early in his career. Some of the hostages were all killed when he was part of a botched operation to get inside of a bank and rescue them from criminals who had armor piercing rounds and explosives.

Several high ranking police officers were fired or demoted, but the Cop was not one of those. There was another situation that the Cop was actually the lead of, just a couple of years before, in which he was able to use snipers to wound two of the hostage takers and kill the leader, freeing all of the hostages safely. He would need to stay clear of the windows. With his experience and training, if anyone knew how to act in a hostage situation, it was him. However, he had to do something quick, before the rest of the people on the floor were evacuated.

The knocking on the door continued to get louder and they threatened to bust down the door. The Cop finally stood up, holding the gun in his right hand, leaning it up against his shoulder with the muzzle beside his head pointed upwards to the ceiling.

"I don't have any weapons," he said as he walked to the door. "I'm not who you want. I hid because I was scared." The Cop's voice betrayed him. His voice was deep and rough, like someone who was very strong and masculine, which he was. It was not a voice that belonged to someone who hid in the bathroom instead of evacuating. He walked to the door and before he began to open it, one of the security guards growled out a phrase that the Cop had uttered or heard so many times that it was cliché, somewhat like a band that had been around for decades, known for one song that they sang repeatedly, until it was what simultaneously what kept them alive and relevant, and at the same time, caused them sickness and emptiness inside: "Come out with your hands up." The real police would be here soon.

Except the real police weren't in a real hurry to get to the hotel room. The police officers in the area, understanding some kind of serious danger in the situation, decided against barging into the hotel, instead trying to make sure the entrance and the lobby was clear and evacuated. They waited for backup.

"The hotel, of course," the Detective muttered under his breath. This is where the shots were coming from this whole time, it made perfect sense. "That's him, that is our guy," yelled the Detective as he ran out of the office, simultaneously trying, and failing, to put his jacket on while being in what could be described as some kind of jogging. He walked through the door of the office, moving through the hallway, before he realized he had forgotten something he might need. He rarely carried it, but it was located in the lower left-hand drawer of his desk. The Detective opened the desk, and removed his gun, put it in his jacket, and then went back through the door, running down the hallway on the way to his car.

The SWAT team assembled outside on the ground as a slightly older and a little more portly man than the rest of them, not wearing the full gear that the others were wearing, gave instruction. "We've got 11 stories to go up, and we have to use the stairs, we don't want to be stuck on the elevator. The room again is 1103..."

The Detective, jogging since getting out of his car, almost breathlessly interrupted. "I've been looking for this guy, let me lead the way, I want him alive, let me go and negotiate with him," he commanded as he showed off his badge to the leader of the Swat team. "This man isn't going down without a fight, he isn't going to surrender," he told the Detective.

"He's clearly not working alone, I think.. I believe that he is the reason behind all the violence and assassinations over the last few weeks. We won't know that if you send your guys up there to go shoot up his body. Let me go, we will get him alive," the Detective yelled in what had become a busy and loud street despite it now being 11:30 at night. The Detective believed that whoever was up there, they were just a part of what had been a basically unheard of time in the City. Whoever was up there could not possibly be the cause of all the mayhem. He must be some kind of pawn, part of a bigger scheme by someone else, reasoned the Detective. He had lied to the man running the SWAT team. The reason it was so important to get him alive was that he wanted to be able to figure out who was behind him. The Detective wasn't prone to conspiracies, he was a very rational man, and went where ever the evidence pointed him. He was also an experienced negotiator, experienced at talking down people from ledges, both metaphorically and literally. This was the only reason that the SWAT team member, someone who had worked with the Detective for quite some time, allowed him to go in, sighing as he explained to the Detective, "He has hostages but he isn't responding to any kind of communication." The Detective pulled out his pistol, and made sure that it was loaded, cocked and the safety was off.

The Detective felt a strange sense of dread as he ran up the stairs, as they refused to take the elevator for obvious reasons, with the SWAT team. With a heavy duty vest like the rest of the team, though he didn't have a helmet, the Detective had the thought that this wasn't him. This isn't what he signed up for, this is what the SWAT team leader signed up for. Someone who was, ironically, actually down at the bottom of the building, directing things. That is what the Detective felt like he should be doing, directing, leading, being the brains. He wanted to be someone who solved mysteries, like in the movies. He wanted be the kind of guy that brought people to justice, by using logic and reason, like he had learned in school. Instead, he was about to have to shoot someone.

The Detective had never fired his gun in the field, but he fired it many times in practice. He was trained, he knew how to do this. He moved his finger to the trigger. He was ready to fire, he was justified. The Cop refused to put his gun down, and he was a murderer. The Detective's finger came back to his hand, and he felt the vibration of the gun. But that was it.

The Detective's body crumpled to the ground awkwardly, lifeless. The Cop's bullet left a hole in his head. The Cop's life didn't last much longer. The SWAT team behind the Detective, all four of them, opened fire with their automatic weapons. Just like the Detective, the Cop was likely dead before he hit the ground.

Chapter 11

The boy fidgeted in one of the front rows of the church as a preacher spoke about what was in front of him. The preacher gave a bible verse, one that the boy didn't pay attention to. The preacher then promised that "the brother" would now say a few words. The preacher stepped down from the podium and walked to the first pew on the left and sat down. A figure walked to the front of the room, something that perked the boy's attention.

"Brothers and Sisters," the unexpected presenter began, as its distinctive voice echoed throughout the now deathly quiet room.

The front lights of the church suddenly flickered, flipping off. Several people in the church gasped, as they were very confused by both the sudden problems with the lights and the person, the thing, that was in front of the room. They knew who the blood brother, the one who was supposed to give the eulogy, was, and whoever was in front of the church, at the podium, was not him. Some of the lights did not come back on, creating an illusion of being a shadowy figure at the front of the room. The one thing that a member sitting in a pew could see, especially if they were in the front half of the room, was that its hands moved to the hood and removed it. The hood was not a part of a jacket common to teenagers, but wasn't quite a traditional religious robe either. The clothing of the uninvited speaker was rather strange, something most of the people at the funeral had never seen before.

After it removed his hood, the boy in the front row swore he could see what it looked like. Its hands, it appeared, weren't hands. They never left the inside of the jacket, and appeared, at least to the kid, that they were more stubs than hands. The face of Ogun frightened the little boy. It appeared to be charred, and black, not necessarily in natural color, as that was entirely unclear and wouldn't have been obvious in the lighting anyway, but as if it had been burned.

From what the kid could see, when it opened its mouth, it didn't seem to have any teeth. The gender of Ogun seemed entirely unclear, and it didn't help when it talked, as it spoke in a somewhat monotone voice that while low, almost hissed, and could have been the voice of a man or a woman. It was impossible to tell whether or not it had breasts thanks to the nature of the clothing.

"What are you, and why are you here?" a large African American man more demanded than asked on in the second row, fighting back tears of rage. The boy in the front, who would swear for the rest of his life that he could see Ogun, told people that he Ogun cracked a very slight and sly smile after the man spoke.

"I am pain," Ogun insisted. "I am the burden, I am the creation of those above you, those that put the man here and now I need you." Ogun's head slightly nodded towards the closed casket in the front of the room, just to make his point painfully obvious. There was a pause, a silence, the sound of nothing. If it wasn't for the sound of a loud fan, the church would have as deathly quiet as the room of dead bodies that the Detective once sat in.

"I just want to serve and protect," Ogun said slowly and sarcastically, though his tone didn't portray it. "Nothing has changed, except what you all know, the pain you now feel. The City has always been like this, controlled by those that are against you. They have created me, and they have created your pain. It is time to make the powerful feel powerless." Ogun clearly didn't want money, unless he could have all of it. Money only interested him because of power, he explained to the audience. Not that he wanted power, he wasn't about to unveil a plan to rule the world, just as he hadn't unveiled a plan to get rich quick. He wanted to take it away. In his eyes, people who had power were dangerous.

Its position of experience, or at least apparent experience, resonated with the crowd. The group had seen a young man die, and the surprise messenger's message of pain, pain caused by others, was something they could both agree with and act upon. This is what caused the neighborhood to fight back, even after the police shootouts with the gang.

Chapter 12

Attempts to reach and reason with the Cop, the man in the hotel room, had failed. As two slain security guards laid to the right of the door, the SWAT team knocked on the door and demanded that he open it. The Cop refused, or at least, they got no answer. The SWAT team kicked down the door, only to find no one in the main room. There was a noise from the back room, covered by a large curtain, so one of the SWAT team members threw a canister of tear gas, which just poisoned the hostages, who made their locations known by coughing after the gas had been thrown, and made them even more miserable, which was a feat in itself considered they were tied up and a couple of them had been beaten.

The Cop was actually in room 1104. He had created a hole in the thin walls between the two rooms and placed the muzzle of his machine gun in the hole. As the SWAT team tear gassed the hostages, who were merely convenient distractions, they walked by his hole, so he pulled the trigger, quickly dropping three of the seven team members. The remaining four, fired wildly at the wall, but most of the shots were too high as the Cop quickly laid on the floor. The Detective, deciding that following the other officers by shooting at the wall wasn't the wisest idea, quickly ran into the hallway, and grabbing the ax designed for fire purposes, knocked enough holes in the door to get through.

As he climbed through, kicking his way through the hole he created, the Cop met him, with his pistol cocked, loaded and pointed at the Detective's head. The Detective raised his gun as well and yelled "drop your weapon." The Cop smiled as the remaining members of the SWAT team assembled in the doorway, with guns pointed at him.

Chapter 13

The murders, the killings, and the attacks continued. They didn't stop with the Cop's death. The City, along with the police, learned, or at least began to think they understood, that the Cop was not the one terrorizing the city. It was someone else instead.

Some citizens were less patient than others. A group of people from a radical and somewhat underground organization, one that had created their own somewhat secret society, a group that believed they could protect themselves without the help of traditional programs, decided to act. They met at the park, in public, unlike the rest of their meetings, and they made it known who they wanted to face, and by the vans and trucks full of machine guns and rifles, how they planned on taking care of the problem. They got their wish. After making plenty of noise, and having the police surround the park, Ogun showed up.

The police, because of the pure volume of weapons, and the already problematic nature of the neighborhood that Ogun had previously been interested in, they weren't going to charge. They weren't going into the park. In fact, the Society had made it clear that any officers who tried to come into the park would be killed. Ogun knew he was who they were looking for, and coming from seemingly nowhere, was in the middle of the protesting group. The muzzles of dozens of guns, many of them automatic weapons were pointed at Ogun, as the Society was almost in a precarious circle, surrounding Ogun.

Ogun, with its hood still on, stopped to speak, "You and I...," he was quickly cut off.

The Society had no patience with him, and wouldn't allow him to speak. A large man, equipped with a red beard so full that he could have been mistaken for a mountain man, someone that wasn't a part of a life that was considered normal or urban, someone that didn't fit into the City, yelled to Ogun in a voice gruff enough to scare most adults "You are the enemy, and this is what we do with enemies."

"That won't work" Ogun responded, almost whispering.

Ogun, who appeared to be holding some kind of home made weapon, fired upon the crowd, but the weapon was pointed more up than directly at anyone. When set off, the device released some kind of needles, long thorn like pieces of sharp metal, into the air, that strangely became inflamed, which caused the vehicles in the park to be set on fire and eventually explode. The trees, and the dry grass were quickly set ablaze as well, causing a mini forest fire in the middle of the City. In response, the crowd fired upon Ogun, but they weren't able to hurt it. Instead, members of the crowd screamed and fired their guns into the air as the needles pierced their skin, and as some of them burned alive. Ogun walked through the flames, slowly, with a gait that spelled triumph. The top of Ogun's hood was burned, with a flame slowly building on its shoulder, but the fire didn't stop Ogun. It would walk past the police perimeter by going through the trees with his dark clothes. No one knew what or where it was.

The police officers had created a perimeter, but all they saw was flames and shadows. It was too dark for them to see what was going on other than the flames. It was like Ogun had disappeared into thin air. They waited to send the firefighters in, because they didn't want to have them fall victim to Ogun as well, and if at all possible, they wanted to catch it. They didn't. The delay, the hesitation, meant that they saved none of the people in the fire. The firefighters mission quickly became a mission of containment, somewhat similar to the mission that the police originally had, but failed to do. They would make sure the fire didn't spread, and eventually put it out and retrieve the charred bodies.

Chapter 14

Some of the people of the neighborhood, this time mainly woman and children, gathered in the street, the same street that was once strewn with bodies, and still stained with blood, with empty casings laying around, and the occasional burn mark from fires. They marched, hand in hand, past the house that burned, and then past the house that of the fallen kid. The police officers in the area got in their cars, and tried to block them from marching further, parking in front of them. They stayed in their cars, and watched as many of the silent protesters walked around the cars, breaking the link between their hands. The rest of them climbed on the police cars, mainly children. As the group of protesters past, probably no more than 60 people, the officers in the four squad cars called for backup and then got out of their cars, heading towards the slow moving protesters, holding no signs and performing no chants. The officers walked from behind them, and tried to start arresting as many as they could, using the traditional plastic zip ties used on protesters.

When some of them resisted, even just moving or laying on the ground, the officers started bating them with nightsticks on the head, even the women and the kids. One officer started spraying as many as he could with mace, running down as many as he could. This caused the crowd to disperse, running every direction, as a couple of more squad cars pulled onto the street, swerving quickly with lights on and sirens blaring, an intimidating sight to the protesters who had been attacked by police in recent weeks.

One of the police officers in the original four cars caught a woman running into a yard and tackled her into the grass. As the officer got up, he reached for his nightstick and then raised it up. The tackled woman reached into the inside of her shirt and gripped her gun that was tucked in her pants. It was a gun that her husband, before his death, kept in the home for protection. Three shots later, the officer cried out in pain and fell to the grass, moaning. This caught the attention of the officers that had just arrived and they came out of their cars with their hand steadied and guns firing. Before the woman could even get up, she was shot several times, laying in someone's yard.

The officers then saw someone in the house behind the woman open up a window. They cautiously moved forward, aiming their guns at the window. The barrel of a shotgun poked its way out and started firing, while most of the officers were still at a distance that it just peppered them, hurting them, but not getting close to killing them.

The firing of the shotgun stopped, but there was no reason to believe that the person behind the window had been hit, as they didn't expose their body at all. Instead, the police believed that he was reloading. The two cops closest to the curb, one that had been hit and was bleeding out of his right arm, sprinted to the front of the door, trying to get inside. Since the door was locked, with multiple locks, thanks to the normal nature of the neighborhood, it wasn't exactly easy to get into. The non wounded officer tried kicking it, screaming in disappointment when it didn't budge. The window shotgun was back, firing up on the officer as he ducked and shot back, missing badly. The officer that had been wounded had wondered around at the right side, the side of the window shooter and was coming back around the backyard. The other officer scrambled on all fours to make it to the left side of the house.

The wounded officer, in serious pain by now, found himself trying to climb a fence in the backyard, in order to get to the back door. After several attempts that only ended in him screaming as his arm continued to bleed and throb, he fell into shock and laid on the grass beside the gate. The other officer had made it to the gate, somehow unwounded, and climbed over rather easily, somewhat puzzled that he wasn't met by the other officer. The rest of the officers stayed back, as though the firing of the shotgun had stopped again, they weren't going to step forward and face the wrath. They could only have their guns drawn, focused on the window and hoped one of the officers from behind the house got there and was able to take him out.

The officer behind the back found a power saw laying in a small shed behind the house, and using an extension cord, started cutting into the door, at least enough to knock it down. The noise caused the shotgun shooter, a short and slender woman to head to the back of the house. The officer had ditched the power saw on the ground and had his gun readied in his hand pointed at the woman. Before he could plead with her to drop her weapon, she pumped it, causing a dramatic and loud metal sound, and pointed it at the officer. So he shot her in the thigh with his pistol, causing her to fall, and fire a shell into the wall before dropping the shotgun.

Chapter 15

The Company was the big business in the City. In many other parts of the nation, the Company is what the City was known for, like when a town is known as the place where a soda was invented, a restaurant was started, or a whole industry was formed. The Company, like most large corporations, did a number of things under the name, and then a number of things with different names and subsidiaries. However, the Company's main focus was vehicular, and more often than not, military vehicles. The City was not where hardly any of the products were produced, it was just where the Company was founded, and where they kept their offices, in a gigantic skyscraper, and in a very traditional manner, a lobby at the bottom, and the executives on top.

Ogun rode the elevator, holding a railroad pick with its right hand on the middle of the rod that the pick was attacked to as the end of the other side rested on the ground. Ogun was looking to get to the top, but the elevator stopped on the 4th floor and a man and a woman prepared to get on. When they looked up from their conversation as the elevator door opened, they saw someone in a hood holding a railroad pick standing alone on the elevator. They decided against getting on, all three of them standing in silence as the man and woman wore surprised looks on their faces with mouths agape and eyes wide. As the elevator closed and went back up, the woman asked, confused, hows such a person would be able to get to the elevator without anyone stopping or noticing in the first place. The idea that it had just walked through the building and the lobby wearing that and having a weapon with it seemed ludicrous. She thought that it must just be some joke that she wasn't in on, that someone in one of the offices had dressed up like the grim reaper and was riding around in the elevator scaring people as a joke, even though it wasn't close to Halloween.

Thanks to the second, or perhaps third depending on how you count it, lock-down of the streets surrounding the neighborhood that Ogun spoke to, and ironically, the recent cuts to the police force, the police were not able to respond to Ogun's invasion of the building very quickly, at least with not large numbers. He was already firmly at the top of the building by the time they were able to respond, which was too late.

As the elevator opened at the top floor, Ogun took a quick step forward and took the pick off of his shoulder, where he had moved it before the door opened, and swung it around, almost spinning it, like he had quite a bit of experience using the tool. A man, a high ranking officer in the company, took a step towards him with a puzzled look on his face, but before he couldn't say anything or even raise his hand at Ogun, the pick hit him in the neck, creating a hole that would soon be fatal wound. Most of the officers in the building had never seen a railroad pick in real life and scattered, screaming, and running away from Ogun, but two of the bigger officers came towards Ogun.

By the time the two were dropped by Ogun and his swinging pick, two overweight security guards came towards it, both with pistols drawn, ready to fire. They came from the left of Ogun, who quickly saw them and moved forward quickly, ducking underneath a desk. While it wasn't exactly fast, clearly walking with a limp, it wasn't exactly immobile. The movement was somewhat strategic, as now, somewhat safe behind a desk, he was between the security guards and the fleeing office members on the floor. Some of the office members thought they would be safe by by hiding in one of the offices with walls made of glass. The first couple of shots by the security guards immediately broke the glass. As the guards continued to fire in the direction of Ogun, a stray bullet hit a woman in the face, causing her body to sprawl across the ground.

The security guards stopped firing because they ran out of bullets in their current clips. There was a pause, and silence, with many of the workers' ears ringing. The sound of a woman crying, followed by the incoherent babbling of man, drifted throughout the room. "He's behind the desk, he's behind the metal desk," yelled another man, presumably to the security guards. This wasn't a revelation, the guards saw him hide behind the desk to start with, but for whatever reason, it caused one of the guards to start firing his now reloaded weapon back at the desk. Ogun remained crouched, somewhat safe behind the desk. The four shots by the guard bounced off the desk, doing nothing. There was another pause. The guard on the left, the one that had not just fired his gun, motioned for the one on the right to split up and circle around, in an attempt to surround Ogun and get to the other side of the desk where they could shoot it.

Despite Ogun seeming unarmed other than the railroad pick, the surviving members of the office remained somewhat huddled in the back of the room, scared to leave or try to run. Ogun heard the security guards try to approach him from behind, thanks to the obvious noise of boots on the floor. It was still somewhat trapped, as if it raised up, it would be the focus of as large of a barrage of gunfire that the mildly trained security guards would be capable of. Then, everyone heard a noise, the noise of the elevator, still active, coming up and stopping at the floor. When Ogun heard the doors opened, he slammed the handle of his pick into the metal desk, creating a loud bang. The bang was followed by the sound of gunfire, including an automatic weapon, a masculine scream, followed by the sound of two objects hitting the floor.

Four security guards had come through the door, jumpy because of the noises heard from floors below, and fired as soon as the door open because of the loud bang created by Ogun. Unfortunately for the security guards, only the two guards trying to sneak around to get Ogun were hit by their gunfire, killing them almost instantly. The new security guards didn't initially know that Ogun was under the desk, but were quickly informed by a shrieking woman in the back corner of the room with makeup running down her face. It didn't seem that it had hit any of the security guards what they had just done, killing the other security guards. Even with a man screaming "What are you doing? You killed them! You killed them!," they didn't seem phased.

Ogun quickly reached into the inside of its clothing and pulled something out. From the vantage point of a man sitting near the huddled masses of what had become basically another hostage situation in the City, it looked like some homemade grenade. Ogun proceeded to hold it with both of its arms and pull its arms out to pull it in half. It then raised its arms just enough above the desk, drawing some quick gun fire from a security guard with the machine gun, to throw the device over the desk, towards the security guards, who were walking forward and had gotten close to the desk. When the two pieces hit the ground, they created minor explosions that spread out shrapnel and sparks that caused mini fires throughout the elevator side of the floor. The explosions knocked the security guards to the floor and wounded them, at least one fatally. The metal desk protected Ogun from most of the blast, except for one long screw that stuck into its back. This didn't seem to bother it much, as it didn't even remove it as it got up. Instead, it walked toward the fires and the now nearly destroyed part of the floor, as the light fixtures had been blown apart by the metal, and there was significant damage, both from the metal and the fires, to the walls. Ogun walked through what had become an image out of a horror or classic slasher movie, towards the security guards laying on the floor. With the railroad pick in its right hand, it found the first guard, a young and fit man now writhing in pain with flames protruding upwards from his back. Ogun immediately swung the pick, putting its left hand on it for support, just like the tool was meant to be used, and came down on the guards head. A man yelled, but it wasn't the man that Ogun killed, as he had no time to scream. A man, one of the top officers in the Company, could barely see what was going on. The fires, along with the desks and other office furniture between the man and Ogun, blocked the man's view from actually seeing the security guard laying on the ground. But, he could see Ogun, and knew exactly what he was doing. The yell was somewhat involuntary, like he was falling, or in a car crash. This surprised even him.

After making sure all the security guards were dead, Ogun calmly and silently attached explosives to the walls. They were originally taped to his body, which made its ability to move even more amazing. They weren't activated at the time of the explosion of his previous bomb that had wounded the security guards, so they weren't in much of a risk of exploding as well, especially since he was behind the desk. He had to move parts of his clothing to get to the ones closer to his thigh and chest, but it was clear that he had enough to blow up the top of the building, or at least the room.

Several of the hostages hatched a plan to get away. Ogun clearly had the elevator blocked, and there wasn't a great reason to trust it to work anyway.

Instead, they focused on the staircase, that was in the middle of the office, on the right hand side, with the door currently closed. Noticing that Ogun didn't move well, they hoped that they could make a run for it and make it down the stairs, knowing that it wouldn't be worth it for Ogun to chase them down the stairs, only to lose the rest of the hostages as well. The man who had previously yelled after Ogun killed the first security guard saw five of his co- workers clearly conspiring to do something. Flat on his stomach, he nodded his head in a way would to signal that they wanted to know what was going on and slowly moved his body towards them. He then whispered, "What are you guys talking about?" "Nothing," one of the women quickly and suspiciously responded. "We are making a run for it," one of the men in the group of five followed up, as the woman shot a glare at him. She was afraid that the longer they waited, and the more people they dragged along, the less likely they would be able to get away, as a large group would clearly grab all of the attention of Ogun. The man in the group, however, believed that the large group would mean that at least some of them would escape. The 6 decided to stagger their escapes out by 5 seconds, just a slow count to 5, long enough that they would not all be in one small group, but short enough that the second half of the group wouldn't be left behind and easy targets.

The first one took off, sprinting to the door, catching Ogun's eye. Ogun, hobbling at this point, took off towards him. The attempted escapee, a rather agile man who made millions on the stock market buying his way into the Company, sprinted as hard as he could, with adrenaline pumping through his veins like it never had before. He beat Ogun to the door rather easily, and went to open the door, only to feel the last feeling of his life, perhaps other than the pain of having his life ended by a railroad pick, a sinking feeling of a plan that had failed. The door was locked.

The woman that followed him was then stuck in a bad place, halfway between the rest of the hostages, and the door. She chose to run back to the rest of the group, but Ogun caught her as she tripped, swinging his weapon with no remorse, taking her life as well.

"You're a monster" yelled one of the hostages, yet another high ranking executive of the Company. Ogun calmly, using what amounted to his hands, took off his hood and screamed "I'm your victim" out of what seemed like a damaged voice box. A nightmare is exactly what the executive thought about when he saw Ogun's face. Clearly the bi-product of some kind of accident, its face was burned, so much that it looks like it should have been fatal, and so much that it looked like it wasn't human, and there was no way to tell the gender. Its cheek bones were sunken in and had holes in them, and it had no hair, either on its head, or where its eyebrows and eyelashes should have been. For some reason, the executive's mind wandered, and he wondered how Ogun had not yet died of infection. It wasn't just the burns that made Ogun hard to look at, so hard to look at, that the executive really only got a 10 second look before finding himself looking away. There was also some kind of metal object that was not only evidently lodged into his skull, but coming out of the right side of his head. One of the executives thought it looked like Frankenstein, though she didn't dare to share this sentiment aloud.

As the day wore on, Ogun saw that a man was talking on his cell phone, and walked up to him, extending out his hand, making it clear that he wanted to see the cell phone. The man hesitated, but as Ogun's eyes stared directly at him, almost to the point where it seemed that they were staring directly into him, which caused the man the man to lose his breath since the eyes did not look human. They had been so damaged and scarred that they almost looked black, and while it was apparent the pupils worked, it never blinked, which looked incredibly painful.

Ogun took the phone from the male secretary, and immediately hit the end button, hanging up the phone from a conversation with the man's wife. Then, clumsily and never removing its fingers from the hood, it pressed the buttons 9-1-1. Putting it on speaker phone after the operator answered after two rings, Ogun greeted the overly perky woman working the other side of the phone not with a customary hello, but with a threat: "If the police try to come into the building in anyway, the building goes down. You know exactly what I am talking about," Ogun said as it finished. Ogun then hung up the phone but kept it in its hands. After trying to do something on the phone for a few minutes, exactly what it was doing wasn't clear to the others, it told one of them to get up, pointing at them with the railroad pick that had been under its arm. It further pointed the pick to the wall, without saying anything, making the hostage stand against the wall. "Next to the bomb," Ogun ordered, as the grown man stood beside it, starting to sob. Ogun then pointed the phone at him, and with the man's eyes closed, the flash and artificial sound of a camera was the next thing the man saw and heard.

"That's a hoax, don't buy into it" a veteran FBI agent yelled at the SWAT team leader. The FBI agent had been shown the picture Ogun took of the man standing next to the bomb. Somehow, Ogun had gotten it trending on several social networking, and the photo was passed around the Internet. Inside, the FBI agent, trained for situations like this, though perhaps unprepared for the evolving Internet impacts of these situations, guessed that it was probably real. Either way, he wasn't about to let people go into the building because he was afraid that it would be blown up by whoever was causing the panic than ran through the City. The skyscrapers all through downtown had been shutdown, and everyone had either gone home, or become one of the thousands of onlookers in the area. The remaining man power when it came to police officers in the City was just trying to keep the crowd back, trying to keep them behind the yellow tape, behind the officers that were supposed to be doing the work to defuse the actual situation.

The truth was, even with the risk of death and millions of dollars in destruction, the officers that were not holding the crowd back were actually bored. They weren't able to communicate with Ogun, they couldn't go in and do anything, they just had to wait, and wait.

The crowd situation quickly unraveled. The crowd had grown into tens of thousands of people, and there seemed to be three main groups, the first being a group that seemed to be protesting Ogun itself, wanting drastic action made for him to be brought down. The second group, one in a similar size, seemed to be Ogun sympathizers, pointing out police cruelty, especially in the neighborhood where the boy had been slain. The third group was smaller and more eccentric, and didn't really seem to have an agenda, other than to just break stuff.

Shots rang out. Someone with a machine gun started firing into the crowd. As screams became more common, the police officers and SWAT team members were forced to try to subdue and infiltrate the crowd. When the latter became impossible thanks to the sheer chaos and trampling of the large amount of people, the officers chose to do the former, firing tear gas canisters into the crowd. The machine gunner didn't stop, continuing to fire his weapon wildly. This caused the police officers to start firing their guns as well, equally as wildly, as they couldn't see anything because of the effects of the many canisters of tear gas thrown.

Chapter 16

The hostage affair dragged into its third day. "They are going to kill you" Ogun whispered to them, slowly, while sitting in a chair, looking out a window. "They are going to kill you!" one of the hostages screamed at him. "Do you think they are going to be able to save you? That they would worry about you surviving, after all this time? To them, you are already dead. You no longer exist."

"Let him set it off," the head FBI agent bellowed. "If he is bluffing, then we catch him, if not, there is nothing we can do anyway, let him kill himself." Looking around at the initially shocked faces around him, he added, "This is the end, it has all come to this, let's bring down the bad guy. He is a gangster, a master of terror, and a thug, and he isn't coming out of this building alive." He was convinced that Ogun was the bad guy, and Ogun was convinced that the FBI Agent was part of what represented the bad guy.

Just like it was commanded to, the police helicopter flew to the side of the building. It would appear that it was dangerously close, but the veteran pilot believed she knew what she was doing. The machine gun operator readied the weapon and had it pointed to the building, looking for any kind of movement. The building had been declared "dead," meaning that salvaging it was not important, and the mission was to solely kill Ogun. It was unspoken, but the other people in the building were considered to be either a part of Ogun or part of the building. Their death, just like the building, was assumed at this point. The machine gun operator's thought process worked a lot like the machine he operated. He had no time for philosophical thoughts about the value of life, whether the utility of Ogun's certain death outweighed the utility of attempting to save others, or if he was living a healthy psychological life. He had orders. He had training. He knew how to operate his tool and believed that the results would lead to good things. It was not something he needed to ponder. He was a man of strength, and action. In one, he had done what his training had taught him to do, to become one with the mission, to become one with the weapon.

The machine gun operator saw something move, which seems almost absurd considering it was night, he was in a helicopter and the building was completely dark. But, he saw something. That was all he needed. He quickly opened fire, spraying into the windows, shattering them. The problem was that, while it was hard to see, he no longer saw anything. At least, not any people. As the machine gun tore mercilessly into the building, a building that took nearly two years to build, a skyscraper, something that was once considered a real feat of humanity, to build something that could reach the sky, but something that was no longer considered anything noteworthy or awe inspiring. The machine gun operator didn't think of this either, he was in the heat of the moment. In fact, he didn't think much about the consequences of his actions to the surroundings around him. This time, it cost him.

Before the helicopter starting firing upon the building, the surviving executives of the building tried to hatch another plan. "We have to do something" one of the top level executives said to the other man. The other man was the CFO, the highest ranking person in the building, the same man that Ogun took a picture of on the wall.

Ogun never seemed to need to sleep, the hostages hadn't even seen it go to the bathroom. It was the only one watching the group of people on the top floor, the rest of the building was understandably empty and because of the threat of bombs, no police officer set foot in the building. It was as if Ogun had allowed the rest of the people to leave, not carrying about those on lower floors. However, because it was alone, sleep would be a huge detriment to holding the remaining people in the building, and they would probably kill it. So it didn't sleep, and it didn't seem to affect it either.

A few of the hostages hadn't slept at all as well, and had gone crazy. This included the CFO, who believed that they should finally just attack Ogun. The problem was, they didn't have any weapons. This is what made the plan seem irrational and desperate, which is exactly what it was. They had to get him when he wasn't looking, when he was distracted with something else.

The police seemed to get impatient and irrational because those in charge of the operation hadn't slept. This was most likely a reason why the FBI Agent gave up on the mission of saving the executives and ordered the attack by helicopter. Of course, a couple of police helicopters had been circling the building off and on, but kept their distance because they didn't want to make it seem like they were attacking the building, and have Ogun set it off. The helicopter that did attack with was more of a military style helicopter, one built for attacking. At that point, the mission had changed.

When the CFO and the other conspiring officer in the office decided to attack Ogun, they used a chair. They had nothing to attack it with, and bringing it down just with their bodies didn't seem to be an option, as Ogun was well built, with broad shoulders and a filled out frame. The CFO was only about average size, while the other man was stocky, short but overweight, out of shape with no natural athleticism. They used the least fancy chair in an otherwise previously elegant room. A simple metal chair, with a plastic backing, but a metal frame, legs and head rest. The plan was for the other man to distract Ogun while the CFO grabbed the chair and beat Ogun repeatedly, enough where he was down on the ground and keep him down. The plan wasn't very well thought out, and they failed.

When the CFO grabbed the chair, which was initially between Ogun and the rest of the hostages, Ogun took a few steps forward and swung his pick, catching the CFO on the face. The other man, who was not able to originally catch Ogun's attention, yelled out a somewhat involuntary yell. Ogun, with his pick still lodged in the CFO's head, walked toward him as the man tried to run away. Knowing that there was no escape, the man starting running in circles, yelling as he backpedaled around the corners, occasionally falling. The absurdity of the man's attempted escape was only matched by, at least for the other hostages, the terror of hearing the CFO scream in pain as he bleed all over the floor from a clearly fatal head wound, especially since there was no medical help to be found.

The other man's fate was sealed, just by the look on Ogun's face, at least from what the man could see. The question was just how. The man ran behind a charred desk, standing behind it, with it separating Ogun and him. However, the desk wasn't very tall, only coming up to the waist of Ogun. The man stood trembling, as Ogun removed the screw that had been in its back since the first day of the hostage situation. Gripping it in its right hand, a hand that was obscured by its sleeve that it never seemed to leave, Ogun inspected it. It was a long screw, one that was once a metallic gray but was now a dark red, resembling dried blood. The man on the other side of the desk stood with his mouth open, shocked that Ogun was able to take it out of itself and still stand up, and not spray blood everywhere. "What are you?" the man asked stunned and stuttering. Ogun tossed the long screw up in the air and caught it, looking at it intently, pausing, dragging what seemed like an inevitable situation out.

Holding the homemade trigger of all of the explosives he set in the building, Ogun raised its arms in a dramatic fashion, and then pushed down the button. The impact was immediate. The walls exploded with the bombs and before the top floor even became inflamed, the ceiling, followed by the roof, collapsed. From ground level, the FBI and police officers could see the explosions rock the top of the building and cause even the outside of the building to catch on fire.

The police helicopter near the building caught on fire as well, and went down quickly, crashing into a building to the right, causing another explosion. The explosion was much fiercer than any on the ground could have predicted, and there was no way that any amount of effort from the fire department could hope to contain. As one officer stood in amazement, mouth and eyes wide open like he had gone into shock, he felt a pinch in his shoulder. It reminded him of an old football injury, one he hadn't thought about in years, or perhaps as if someone had walked behind him and squeezed the extra skin on the top of his shoulder. He was sure that it was the latter, at least as sure as one could be about anything in a split second, like an instinctive expectation. He turned his face, which was glowingly hot thanks to the raging fire above, to look to see who was behind him. No one was close enough to have pinched him or grabbed him, but he did see something. A long nail stuck into his shoulder, something that apparently came from the blast. As he looked around, he saw that many around him had similar wounds, that they were coming from the blast above.

As the building went ablaze with explosions that not only rocked the night sky, but the buildings around it as well, a father, standing a safe distance away at ground level, hugged his young son. "It's over now right?" the son asked. "The good guys won, right? Dad, this happened for a reason didn't it"? The father paused and extended his arms to hold his son's face right in front of his, so the two's foreheads met. He paused and then finally whispered, stammering, "I—I don't know."

The End

Clint Hulsey is an English teacher in Texas, with a degree in Philosophy from the University of North Texas. He spends his spare time watching as many movies as he can, playing as many games as possible, and reading as many books as his eyes will allow him. He also tells a few jokes that no one laughs at and enjoys the occasional baseball game.

www.ingramcontent.com/pod-product-compliance
Lightning Source LLC
Chambersburg PA
CBHW051346020726
47501CB00007B/2304